Robert
and the Great
Pepperoni

Also by Barbara Seuling

Oh No, It's Robert

Robert and the Attack of the Giant Tarantula

Robert and the Snake Escape

Robert and the Great Pepperoni

by Barbara Seuling
Illustrated by Paul Brewer

A
LITTLE APPLE
PAPERBACK

SCHOLASTIC INC.

New York   Toronto   London   Auckland   Sydney
Mexico City   New Delhi   Hong Kong   Buenos Aires

ISBN 0-439-23547-2

12 11 10 9 8   4 5 6/0

Printed in the U.S.A.
First Scholastic printing, November 2001

For my friend Kyle Mulloy
—B. S.

To Barbara, thanks for Robert
—P. B.

Contents

Climbing Mountains   1

Up a Tree   6

Fake Ice Cream   11

A Matter of Life or Death   16

The Deal   20

Second Thoughts?   26

The Great Pepperoni   30

Deep, Deep Trouble   37

The Photo   43

Mount Everest, Here I Come!   49

A Home for Pepperoni   56

Robert and the Great Pepperoni

Permission Slip
I give permission for
my son/daughter
x _____
to go on a class trip
to Forest Park.

Climbing
Mountains

"**S**ettle down, children," said Mrs. Bernthal to the class one morning. "I have good news. We're going on a trip."

A class trip! Robert closed his eyes and tried to send his thoughts to Mrs. Bernthal by mental telepathy. *Dinosaurs. Please, please let it be dinosaurs.* The natural history museum had a new exhibit he was dying to see. His best friend, Paul, was probably wishing just as hard for the planetarium. Paul loved anything to do with space.

"We are going to be one of the first classes to use the new climbing wall in Forest Park," said Mrs. Bernthal, clasping her hands in front of her.

Robert frowned and opened his eyes.

"What's a climbing wall?" called out Lester Willis.

"It's like the side of a very steep mountain. It has finger- and toeholds, and you have to make your way up the wall," said Susanne Lee Rodgers.

"What if you fall?" asked Melissa Thurm. Melissa was afraid of everything.

"You won't fall," said Mrs. Bernthal. "You'll wear a harness that will keep you from falling."

"When are we going?" asked Kevin Kransky.

"A week from next Wednesday," said Mrs. Bernthal. "Have your parents sign this permission form and bring it in by Friday—a week from today." She went around the room handing out slips of paper.

"The climbing wall sounds like fun," said Robert as he and Paul walked home together. They almost always walked, unless it rained. Then they rode the school bus.

"I saw a National Geographic special on mountain climbing," said Paul. "A man got killed. He fell a gazillion feet down the mountain."

"You think the wall's dangerous?" asked Robert.

"They wouldn't let us go if it was. Would they? Let's look at the permission slip."

Robert pulled his permission slip out of his notebook. He read it out loud.

"I give permission for my son/daughter _____ *to go on a class trip to Forest Park."*

"Farther down," said Paul. "Look." He pointed to the lines at the bottom.

"I will not hold the school responsible for any injury or death that may result from an accident during the trip."

"Injury! Death! It *is* dangerous!"

Paul scratched his head. "But Mrs. Bernthal wouldn't let us do anything that could hurt us."

"Then why do our parents have to sign this?" asked Robert.

"It's probably something the school has to do," said Paul.

"Maybe." Robert wished he could get the picture of the man falling down the mountain out of his head.

Up a Tree

Robert was cat-sitting for Ms. Laney over the weekend. He stopped at her house on his way home. He opened the front door with the key she had given him. Ginger came right up to him with a big *meow*.

Ms. Laney had left three cans of food on the kitchen counter. Robert opened one of the cans and dumped the contents into Ginger's dish. Ginger went right to it when Robert put it down. Then he filled her water dish with fresh water.

While Ginger ate, Robert went out the back door to the yard. He saw a big yellow dog on the other side of the fence. A doghouse stood in the corner of the yard.

"Hi," he said, walking over to the fence.

The dog was on a chain. Its tail wagged furiously. It came over and nuzzled Robert's fingers through the fence with its big pink nose.

Robert looked at the dog's tags. There was one tag to show it had its rabies shot. Another one had a telephone number, but no name.

The dog was skinny. Robert searched in his pockets for some kind of food, but all he came up with was a red gummy bear covered with fuzz.

"I have to go now," he said, scratching behind the dog's ears. Robert went back to the house to lock up. But as he opened the back door, Ginger zoomed out.

"Hey!" cried Robert. He ran after her, but the cat climbed up the big apple tree in the yard. She looked down at him from a branch that was way out of reach.

A ladder rested against the tree. Was it for picking apples in the fall, or did Ginger always climb trees? Robert wondered. He started to climb the ladder. On the fourth rung, his legs felt shaky. He let himself down, one rung at a time. When his feet were on the ground again, he felt better.

"Here, Ginger, here, kitty kitty," Robert called. The cat did not move. What should he do? He knew he couldn't leave her there.

Robert went into the house and called his mother. "Stay there," she said. "I'll be right over." Robert sat on the step. Over in the next yard, the yellow dog stared at him through the fence.

Robert's mom had no trouble climbing the ladder. She picked up the cat and climbed back down.

Once Ginger was safely in the house again, Robert walked home with his mom. He told her what had happened on the ladder. "It looked so easy," he said, "until I got up to the fourth rung."

"It's nothing to worry about, Rob," his mom said. "Ladders can feel pretty shaky if you've never been on one."

But if a ladder felt shaky, how would a climbing wall feel?

Fake Ice Cream

Mrs. Bernthal asked everyone in room 204 to bring something to share with the class that had to do with rock climbing.

Charlie, Robert's older brother, had told Robert to take a hanky, in case he had a nosebleed. Robert knew that Charlie liked to tease him, so he didn't listen. Instead he brought a book with lots of pictures of rocks and minerals.

Paul brought a plastic bag and a marker. "Rock climbers use these for collecting specimens," he said.

11

"What specimens?" asked Matt Blakey. "It's a climbing wall, not real rocks."

"Yes, Matt, that's true," said Mrs. Bernthal. "But there's nothing wrong with pretending. Thank you, Paul."

Susanne Lee brought survival food. "Astronauts eat this kind of food, too," she explained. "It doesn't weigh much or take up much room, so it's good for long trips to places where you might not find food."

She opened a silver-colored pouch. "This is strawberry ice cream," she said, showing the class. Inside the pouch were dry brown cubes. They didn't look anything like strawberry ice cream.

Susanne Lee broke up the cubes into tiny pieces so everyone could have a taste. Robert made a face as he touched his sample with the tip of his tongue. Hmmm. It tasted good. He licked it again. It really did taste like strawberry ice cream!

He put the rest of the sample in his mouth
and ate it. Maybe a pocketful of those cubes
would be fun to take along on a rock-climbing
trip. Susanne Lee knew everything.

The trip to the climbing wall was still a week away. Robert wanted to go, but he kept thinking of his shaky knees on that ladder. Should he tell Mrs. Bernthal? What if she made him stay home?

When he got home from school, Robert's mom was on the phone. She sounded pretty upset. "Don't go near it if it comes back," she said into the telephone.

Robert happened to look out the window at their yard. A big yellow dog was sniffing the grass. "Mom!" he called.

"It could be sick or carrying a disease," his mom said into the phone.

"Mom!" Robert said again.

"Just a minute, Robert," said Mrs. Dorfman while she held her hand over the receiver. "I'm talking on the phone."

"I know, but . . ." Robert's mom signaled to him to be quiet. She continued her conversation. Robert went out to the yard.

The dog came right up to him and licked his hand. Robert scratched behind the dog's ears.

"Robert!" cried his mom moments later, opening the door to the yard. "Be careful! That must be the stray dog Mrs. Rudner called me about. He could be dangerous!"

"That's what I was trying to tell you," said Robert, bending down and holding out his hand. "I know this dog. It's the one that was chained up next door to Ms. Laney's."

A Matter of Life or Death

Robert looked at the dog's collar. The tags were gone, including the one with the phone number. Maybe the dog's chain had broken and the tags had fallen off. "I wonder how he got loose," Robert said.

"I'll call the sheriff," Robert's mom said as she went inside. "He'll know what to do."

The dog was still in the yard, lying at Robert's feet, when the sheriff arrived. He wagged his tail as the sheriff approached.

"Several people in the area have called about this dog," said the sheriff to Mrs.

Dorfman. "He belongs to Sam Pratt. Sam says he doesn't want him back. Said we might as well shoot him."

"*Shoot* him?" cried Robert, holding on to the dog. "You can't do that!"

"It would be a shame," said the sheriff. "He seems like a nice enough dog. Let's see if the animal shelter can take him."

Robert knew about the shelter. They tried their best to find homes for unwanted animals. But if they had no room or couldn't find homes for them, they put animals to sleep. *Forever.*

The sheriff went over to his car and called something in on the radio.

"Mom, can he really shoot the dog?" Robert asked.

"I don't know, Rob."

The sheriff came back. "Well," he said, "the shelter is full. They'll clean him up and give him his shots so they can place

him in a foster home, but they have to find one right away. They can keep him overnight, but that's all."

"What's a foster home?" asked Robert.

"A family that will take care of the dog until they find him a permanent home."

Robert looked at his mom hopefully.

"No," she said. "No dogs, Robert."

Robert sighed. It was the same old story. He could take care of other people's pets, and even have pets of his own if they were neat and tidy and could be kept in his room. But that did not include dogs.

The sheriff took the dog by the collar and led him away.

The Deal

Robert could usually eat two burritos. That night he could barely finish one. He even skipped the chocolate pudding with whipped cream on top for dessert. He fed Fuzzy, his tarantula, and Flo and Billie, his doves. Then he did his homework and went to bed early.

His parents came in together to say good night. It had been a long time since both his mom *and* dad had tucked him in.

"Rob?"

"Mmmm?"

"Rob, your father and I want to talk to you."

"Okay." He sat up.

"It's about that dog."

Robert sat up straighter. "What about him?"

"We've been talking," said his mom. "Your father and I agree that you have been an excellent pet-sitter."

"Excellent," his father repeated.

Robert's heart beat faster.

"And you kept your promise about the bunnies," said his mother.

Robert thought back to when he'd taken care of a stray bunny that had babies. He'd promised his mom he would take them to the animal shelter if he couldn't find homes for them. Luckily, the rabbits were rescued by their owner before they had to be put to sleep.

"We feel you deserve something special for your hard work," said Mr. Dorfman.

What were they trying to say? Robert thought he would pop if they didn't hurry up and tell him.

"If you want to take in that dog until he is adopted, it's okay with us," said his mom.

Robert rubbed his eyes. Was he asleep and dreaming? He couldn't believe it.

"We will all try really hard to get along with this idea." Mrs. Dorfman looked at her husband. Mr. Dorfman looked uncertain, but he didn't object.

"And you'll have to do your part," Robert's dad added.

"What's my part?"

"You'll have to train the dog so he is adoptable."

"Okay."

"This is temporary. You will have to give him up when the time comes. You understand that, don't you?"

Robert remembered the dog's cold nose on his fingers. He remembered the dog's brown eyes that sparkled when he petted him. Most dogs didn't grin, but this one did, whenever he saw Robert.

"Yes, yes!" he said. He finally had a dog. A real, live dog!

The next day after Robert got out of school, all three of them went to the animal shelter to get the dog. A man in a white lab coat brought the dog out. The dog's tail wagged when he spotted Robert.

"I'm Dr. Hudson," said the vet. "You've got a healthy dog here. He's been cleaned up and he's got all his shots."

As they started to leave the vet's office, the dog lifted his leg on Dr. Hudson. Robert gasped.

"I guess he's not housebroken," said Dr. Hudson. "You're going to have to work on

this guy. He's old for adoption—he's about two. You've got to make him adoptable."

"What does that mean, exactly?" asked Robert.

"It means he must go to the bathroom *outdoors*." Dr. Hudson looked down at his pants. "It means he can't chew and destroy things that are not his. He must understand simple commands like 'sit' and 'stay.' He should also recognize his name and come when he's called." The vet bent down to pat the dog. "What did you say his name was?"

"I didn't," said Robert. "We don't have a name for him yet."

"Well," Dr. Hudson said, "as I remember, Sam just called him 'Dog.' When you give him a real name and he starts to understand it, it will be easier to train him."

"Okay."

"Don't forget the housebreaking," said Dr. Hudson.

Second Thoughts?

Mr. Dorfman had hardly opened the door before the dog pulled Robert past him and inside.

"Hey! I'm supposed to be pulling you!" said Robert.

The dog sniffed the corner of Mr. Dorfman's leather recliner and lifted his leg.

"No!" cried Robert and Mr. Dorfman at the same time. But it was too late.

Robert saw a little vein in his dad's neck pop out. His mom's hands went to her cheeks as the dog's tail swept over the coffee table, barely missing a crystal polar bear.

"I'll take him out," said Robert before anyone told him to. He and the dog dashed out the back door and into the yard.

Robert let the dog off the leash. The dog went right to a bush at the far end of the yard and sniffed all around it.

This was not going to be easy, Robert thought. He had to work fast, or his parents might have second thoughts about being a foster family.

That evening Robert took the dog out to the yard every hour, with broken dog biscuits jammed in his pocket. He read once that dogs should be rewarded with treats or pats every time they did something right.

By ten o'clock, Robert was so tired he could hardly move his feet up the stairs to

his room. He got into his pajamas and was just about to spread newspapers over the floor, when the dog lifted his leg on Robert's beanbag chair, the one he and Paul always sat in.

"NO!" Robert screamed. He grabbed the dog by the collar and, barefoot, dragged him downstairs and into the yard. The dog was so startled his ears were flattened against his head. He whimpered.

"I'm sorry, boy," Robert said, scratching the dog behind the ears. The grass was cold and wet on Robert's bare feet. "It's not your fault. But we are going to be in big trouble if you don't get housebroken soon."

The dog nuzzled Robert's hand. They went back inside. Robert wished on a star that night. He crossed his fingers, too.

The Great Pepperoni

The next morning Robert dragged himself out of bed. He put his foot over the side and it landed on something soft and furry.

It wasn't a dream! There really was a dog in his room. The dog was looking up at Robert and wagging his tail. Robert held his breath as he looked for signs of puddles. There were none! The newspapers were dry.

"Does he have a name?" asked Charlie, coming into his room. He threw a rubber ball to the dog. The dog jumped as the ball hit him on the nose.

"Not yet," said Robert.

"Well," said Charlie, "this dog can really handle a ball."

"He . . . he'll learn." Robert wished he could go back to bed.

"Yeah, and you'll pitch for the Yankees next year!" Charlie teased. Robert wasn't very good at most sports.

Then Charlie bounced the ball off Robert's head.

"Hey!" yelled Robert.

The dog stood up and barked at Charlie. Charlie jumped back. "Okay, okay!" he said, leaving Robert's room.

Robert turned around just in time to see the dog lifting his leg on the wall.

"Oh, no!" he cried. If only he had taken him outside right away. Robert dressed in a hurry and brought the dog down to the yard. He filled a bowl with water and put it on the ground. He went off to school with sleep still in his eyes.

That morning Mrs. Bernthal talked more about the wall-climbing trip. Robert tried to pay attention, but he kept daydreaming about what he would name the dog. He wrote one name after another in his notebook and showed it to Paul. *Rex. Rocky. Homer. Bones.* None of them seemed right.

Coming home was just as he dreamed it would be. The second he walked into the yard, the dog ran up to him and slobbered him with kisses. His tail worked back and forth like the windshield wipers on Mr. Dorfman's car.

Homework could wait. It was Friday. Robert stayed in the yard and he and the dog played tug-of-war with a stick. Then Robert practiced the "sit," "lie down," and

"stay" commands. Each time the dog got it right, Robert gave him a small piece of dog biscuit.

"Stay" was the hardest. Every time Robert walked away, the dog got up to follow him.

After a while they went in. Robert's mom and dad were looking at the paper. Charlie was messing with the VCR. They were waiting for the pizza to arrive. Friday night was always pizza night, and they usually watched a video together.

"Where is that pizza?" said Mr. Dorfman, checking his watch.

Robert's mom read the box from the videotape Charlie chose. "*The Attack of the Aliens.* Don't you guys ever choose anything that isn't silly or disgusting?"

The doorbell rang. The dog jumped up and barked.

"Well, he's a good watchdog, anyway," said Robert's mom as she answered the door. She paid the deliveryman and brought in the box of pizza.

The dog nearly went berserk. He ran in circles. He whined. He panted. He looked like he would explode at any second.

"Mom, he's hungry," said Charlie.

"He can't be," said Robert's mom. "He ate a whole bowl of dog food earlier." She put the pizza box down on the dining room table.

The dog stared up at the pizza box, drooling.

"He sure knows about pizza," said Robert, sitting down at the table. He opened the box, tore a tiny piece off the pizza, and tossed it to the dog. The dog swallowed it whole.

"Sit!" said Robert. The dog sat. Robert tossed him a piece of pepperoni off the pizza. "Good boy!" he said, scratching the dog behind his ears.

"It's not good to feed the dog from the table," said Mr. Dorfman. He cut up his slice with a knife and fork.

Robert was pretty hungry himself. He bit into his slice. The dog drooled, watching him.

"I've got it! Pepperoni!" he shouted.

"Yes, it is," said his mom. "Isn't that what you always ask for?"

"Not the pizza! The dog! Pepperoni! That's his name!"

"The Great Pepperoni! It sounds like a magic act," said Charlie.

Pepperoni's tail thumped on the floor. Robert tossed him another bite of his slice. His dad frowned.

"Oops. I'm sorry," said Robert.

"Well," said Robert's mom, "I hope one of the first things you do is make his mistakes disappear."

"I'll train him with pizza!" said Robert.

"What happens when you run out of pizza?" asked Charlie.

"I guess I'll have to get more."

Pepperoni barked. He seemed to think that was a fine idea.

Deep, Deep Trouble

On Saturday the newspapers on the floor in Robert's room were dry again. Robert didn't wait to get dressed. He put on his slippers. "Come on, Pepperoni," he called.

He ran downstairs with Pepperoni at his heels and grabbed a plastic bag filled with leftover pizza cut up into small bites. The minute they were in the yard, Pepperoni lifted his leg against the fence.

"Good dog!" yelled Robert. He ran over to Pepperoni and gave him a piece of pizza. He scratched his ears. He kissed his face. "Oh, please," Robert begged. "Please be housebroken!" Pepperoni wagged his tail as if he understood.

Later that day Robert was in his room on his beanbag chair reading a book about mountain climbing. Pepperoni lay across his feet. The book had pictures of people on ropes hanging by their fingertips over great canyons. He imagined himself dangling on the ropes as rocks tumbled down all around him.

"Robert!"

His father's voice broke his concentration. He put the book down and went to the window overlooking the yard.

"What, Dad?"

"I think you'd better get down here," he answered. "This yard is becoming a minefield of dog pretzels."

Robert thumped down the stairs in his sneakers and went out to the yard. His dad was wiping something off his shoe.

"Oh," he said, understanding what the problem was. He went inside to look for plastic bags.

The bags came in all sizes. Robert was sure the snack size would be too small. The gallon size was too big. He took one quart size and one sandwich size.

Robert picked up all the dog pretzels he could find. He wished he had a third hand to hold his nose while he used his other hands to scoop and bag. Now he knew that having a dog had its downside.

On Monday, Robert dressed in a hurry. Pepperoni watched him. "Hold on, boy." They made it to the yard without an accident. Robert hugged Pepperoni extra hard before he left for school.

Robert was glad his mom had made arrangements with her partner at the travel agency to do some of her work from home. While she worked in her little office upstairs, Pepperoni had company. And when Robert got home from school, it was nice to know his mom was there.

At twenty past three, the school bus stopped on Robert's corner. He got off. He'd taken the bus so he could get home to Pepperoni faster. He unlatched the backyard gate, but Pepperoni wasn't there. He went into the house.

"Mom? Where's Pepperoni?"

Mrs. Dorfman came out of her upstairs office and stood at the top of the stairs. She took off her glasses.

"Pepperoni is in the upstairs bathroom," she told him. "He's being punished."

"Why? What did he do?" Robert asked.

"He dug up my flower bed. There are deep trenches where my petunias used to be." She didn't yell. She spoke calmly, but her hair was coming undone.

The bathroom looked like a snowstorm had hit it. Toilet paper was everywhere. Some of it was shredded. Some was draped on Pepperoni. Pepperoni's mouth was bright red.

"Pepperoni! What did you do?" Robert saw his mom's makeup bag on the floor, with the lipstick container open and empty. Pepperoni must have eaten the lipstick part. As Robert straightened the fluffy blue bath mat, he saw that it had been chewed up.

"Oh, no." Robert sank down onto the floor. He tried to clean the lipstick off Pepperoni's mouth, but Pepperoni still looked like a circus clown. He climbed on Robert and covered him with wet kisses.

After he cleaned up the mess, Robert took Pepperoni downstairs into the yard.

"How can I make you understand?" he said as the dog nuzzled his hand. "We are in deep, deep trouble!"

This card certifies that *Pepperoni* the dog is officially **HOUSEBROKEN.**

The Photo

"Pepperoni is housebroken, I think," said Robert as he and Paul ate their lunch the next day.

"That's great," said Paul.

Robert yawned. He had spent yesterday afternoon helping his mom fix the flower beds that were ruined. He picked up dog pretzels with his new pooper-scooper. After dinner and homework, he practiced his commands with Pepperoni.

"So what can he do now?" asked Paul.

"He can sit, and stay, and lie down," said Robert. "I can't get him to roll over, but I'm working on it."

"Does he come when you call him?"

"No," Robert said, disappointed. "He doesn't seem to get that."

"Even when you feed him pizza?"

"Even when I feed him pizza," said Robert.

"Well, I think you did a lot," said Paul. "He's a great dog, and it sounds like he almost always behaves."

"I guess," said Robert. The way Paul said it, it didn't sound so bad. Then he remembered his mom's face when she'd told him about her petunias.

"My parents have been really good," he said. "But I never know what's going to happen next. If Pepperoni does anything like chewing something or digging up the flower bed again, they're going to crack."

Robert had heard that line in a movie. It seemed to fit right now.

Before they went home, Mrs. Bernthal reminded them about the class trip the next day. "Remember to wear shoes with rubber soles that have a good grip," she said. "And bring lunch and snacks. We'll be out most of the day."

When Robert got home, Pepperoni was curled up on his bed. He flopped down next to the dog and buried his head in Pepperoni's fur.

Robert's mom knocked. "Phone call for you, Rob," she said. "It's someone named Annie, over at the animal shelter."

Robert picked up the phone in the upstairs hall. "Hello?"

"How are you doing with your dog?" Annie asked.

"He has a name now. Pepperoni."

"That's a neat name," said Annie. "And how is Pepperoni doing?"

Robert told her everything Pepperoni had learned. He didn't want Annie to think he wasn't doing his job. "I've been training him with pizza."

"Wonderful," said Annie. "Do you think he's adoptable?"

"Oh . . . I . . . don't know," said Robert. The question surprised him. He needed more time.

"Well, here's the thing. We thought we'd put a picture of Pepperoni in the local paper. If we show his picture and say something nice about him, someone may be interested in adopting him."

"Okay," said Robert. "I'll take his picture."

"Great. Take a few shots, if you can. We'll need them by Friday to get in the next issue. We'll put one in that really shows him off as something special. Don't worry. It sounds like you're doing a great job. Someone is going to get a terrific dog."

Yes. Someone is. Robert just wished he were the someone.

Robert had an almost full roll of film in his camera, and that night, he used it up on Pepperoni. He took pictures of Pepperoni sitting, standing, lying down, sleeping, and eating. He took pictures of Pepperoni on his bed, in the yard, and under the coffee table in the living room.

Finally, feeling tired and silly, he started dressing Pepperoni up for the last few pictures. Charlie walked by and joined in. First Pepperoni wore Charlie's Yankees baseball cap and then he wore Robert's earmuffs. Next they put Mom's sunglasses on him and dressed him in Dad's barbecue apron and chef's hat. They laughed until

their sides were sore. Even Pepperoni
seemed to be laughing as he rolled over on
his back for a belly rub.

Mount Everest, Here I Come!

The class was in high spirits on the bus to Forest Park. The girls, as usual, started to sing. The boys, as usual, pretended they couldn't stand the noise.

"Quack, quack, quaaaaack!" croaked Lester Willis, flapping his arms like wings. The other boys covered their ears and made faces.

Robert and Paul ignored the noise and compared sneakers. They had made sure to follow Mrs. Bernthal's instructions about what shoes to wear. Paul's had a lot of spiky things on the bottom. Robert's had treads like car tires.

At Forest Park, a guide led the class to the climbing wall. He wore a brown ranger's hat and a green uniform. The words *Park Service* were sewn on his sleeve.

"It's thirty feet tall," he told them, "or about three stories high. There are finger- and toeholds built into it. They are small— some of them too small for much of a grip—but the challenge is to find a hold and get enough leverage to help you advance up the wall. You will be wearing a harness that's attached to the wall by a rope when you climb, so you won't get hurt if you slip. Two of you can climb at the same time. Just follow my instructions. You have to trust me."

Robert waited his turn in line. He watched as Paul, in front of him, put the harness on. He felt a little like he would throw up as he moved to the first place in line. That wall looked pretty high, and it was straight up. Mountains were on a slant, weren't they? He could hardly see the finger- and toeholds from where he stood.

Now Matt Blakey was on the wall. He seemed to be in a hurry to get to the top.

"Slow down," the guide called to Matt. "Think about each step carefully."

Paul was halfway up the wall.

"That's right, son, you've got it," the guide called after him.

Robert thought about what the guide had said. You had to trust him to climb the wall. That's how Pepperoni learned, by trusting Robert. They took one step at a time. Robert trusted the guide. He would do just what he said, and think about each move he made.

"Oops!" Matt lost his footing. He swung in the harness until he got his footing again. Well, at least you couldn't fall off the wall and get killed.

Paul was down on the ground again. He got out of the harness and gave Robert a thumbs-up. The guide helped Robert into the harness next. "Way to go, Robert!" called Lester. Robert tried to smile, to show he wasn't afraid.

"All right," said the guide. "Find a place on the wall you can grab onto with your right hand."

Robert felt around with his fingers. He stretched way to the right and up. He found a place where his fingers fit into a small space. He held on.

"Now find a place for your left foot," said the guide.

The toe of Robert's sneaker scraped the wall until he found one.

"Now find another hold for your left hand, and then your other foot."

Robert swallowed hard and concentrated. He lifted his foot off the ground. He held on as he searched the wall with his toe. One place was too small. He needed a better place to put his toe. He found it.

"Good. You've got the idea," said the guide. "Keep going, one move at a time."

Robert found one toehold or fingerhold after another and started his way up the wall. At one point, his knees began to tremble. Robert remembered his mom telling him it was natural to be a little shaky on the ladder because he had never used one before. He had never been on a climbing wall before, either. He kept going. Soon his knees stopped shaking.

When he reached the top, Robert felt so good he looked down at his classmates on the ground.

"Don't look," called the guide. Robert knew why he said that. Robert's head swam

and he had to close his eyes to stop being dizzy. "Climb down just as you climbed up," said the guide. "One step at a time."

Robert eased down, his fingers and toes searching for one place after another. The rope was right there, attached to his harness. He knew it would save him from falling if he slipped. At last one foot landed on the ground. Robert jumped off the wall. His knees felt like jelly, but he had done it.

On the bus ride back to school the girls were too tired even to sing, and the boys were quiet, too. Robert couldn't wait to tell his parents that he had climbed the wall. And to curl up with Pepperoni.

A Home for Pepperoni

More than a week had gone by. When Robert got home from school, Pepperoni greeted him with his tail wagging. His parents weren't there, but the house didn't seem so empty now.

Robert noticed a note from his mom on the kitchen table.

Rob,

Had to run over to the mall to pick up some papers from the office. Be right back.

Mom

The latest issue of *The Guide,* a free local paper, lay on the kitchen table with the rest of the mail. He opened it to the section where pets were offered for sale or adoption.

"Look!" he shouted, forgetting that no one was around. Pepperoni's picture, in the apron and chef's hat, was at the top of the page. Robert read out loud: *"Yellow Lab mix. Good family dog. Pepperoni loves pizza and is affectionate and gentle."* Robert never expected them to use one of the silly pictures. Wait until Charlie saw it!

Now all they had to do was wait and see if anyone responded.

Upstairs, Robert dropped his book bag from his shoulder. Friday! He had all weekend to ride his bike and play with Pepperoni.

The phone rang. Robert picked up the extension in the hall. It was Annie.

"A man named Pietro Gardini saw Pepperoni's picture," she said. "Can we come over this evening so he can meet Pepperoni?"

Robert's stomach twisted into one big knot. It was too soon. He needed more time with Pepperoni. He still had to teach him to come when he called his name. He still had to buy him that huge rawhide bone he had seen in the pet store. He still had to make Pepperoni a perfect dog, so he would find the perfect home.

"My parents aren't here now," he said. "But I guess it's okay." He wished he could just say, "No! I'm not ready!" but he couldn't.

"Okay, thanks," said Annie. "We'll be over around eight o'clock. Tell your parents when they come home."

"Okay, I will." Robert hung up, dragged himself into his room, and sank into his beanbag chair. Pepperoni lay at his feet, his chin resting on Robert's sneakers. They stayed that way for a long time.

Shortly after the pizza was finished and the video of *Doctor Slime* had been put in the VCR, the doorbell rang. Pepperoni barked, and Mrs. Dorfman got up to open the door.

"Come in, please," she said, showing them in. "It's so nice to meet you, Mr. Gardini."

"Please call me Pete," he said, extending a hand. Mrs. Dorfman shook it and smiled.

"Ah, and this must be Pepperoni!" Pete got down on one knee. Pepperoni gave him a slobbery kiss. "I think we are going to be friends." Robert felt a little jealous.

Mr. Dorfman showed Annie and Pete to the dining room, and they sat down.

"I am opening a new restaurant," Pete said, "on Route 4. Pete's Pizza Palace. I want people to come there with the whole

family. When I saw Pepperoni's picture, with the hat and the apron, and read that he loves pizza, it gave me an idea."

Pete leaned over and smiled. "I will use this dog for my logo."

"What's a logo?" asked Robert, glancing at Annie. She winked at him. Maybe she didn't know what it was, either.

"It's a picture or a symbol. My logo will be a picture of a dog in a chef's hat and an apron. We will put it in all our ads and on our napkins and pizza boxes. People will see it and know that my restaurant is a friendly place where they can bring the whole family."

Robert frowned. "But where will Pepperoni *live*?"

Pete stopped smiling. "Oh, no," he said. "I'm sorry. I gave you the wrong impression. I want the dog for my family. We lost our dog, Pavarotti, about a month ago."

Pete's voice got sad. "He was fourteen years old, part of our family. My wife and children cried for days. When I saw the picture of Pepperoni in the paper, I thought he would make a good dog for my

family. It was after we decided to adopt him that I got the idea for the logo. I kept looking at the picture. It made me laugh."

Robert felt better. He liked Pete. He knew he and Pepperoni would get along just fine. Pete's family was probably pretty nice, too. But he didn't feel ready to give up his dog.

His dog! Robert had never thought of Pepperoni as his dog before. He loved him, and he loved having him around, but he always knew Pepperoni would someday have a different owner.

"Pete, are you ready to take him now?" asked Annie.

Robert almost stopped breathing.

"Yes, that would be fine. He can come home with me tonight. My family will be so happy."

Robert got up. "Excuse me. I need a drink of water." He went to the kitchen. Pepperoni followed him. He got down on the floor and let the dog slobber him with kisses. He hugged him hard, scratching behind his ears. "I love you, Pepperoni," he whispered into the dog's ear. Pepperoni licked his nose.

"Pepperoni," called Annie. The dog's ears perked up. "Come here, boy." Robert let go and Pepperoni bounced into the living room. Robert followed him, his mouth open.

"He did it!" he said.

"Did what?" asked Annie.

"He came when you called his name. He's never done that before!"

Annie and Pete looked up from some papers. "Ah, you have done a great job," said Pete. "Annie just told me you trained him to be a good dog."

It was hard to speak. "Can I . . . would it be okay . . ." Robert couldn't get it out.

"Of course. Come to visit Pepperoni anytime," said Pete. "We would like that. Here is our address." He wrote something on a card and handed it to Robert. Then he reached into his jacket pocket. "And always, there will be a big welcome for you when you visit my restaurant." He handed a couple of coupons to Mrs. Dorfman.

"Free pizza!" she exclaimed. "How nice!"

Annie and Pete were ready to leave. Pepperoni looked confused.

"You're going with Pete," said Robert. "I'll see you soon." He gave Pepperoni's ears one last scratch. "And I'll bring you that rawhide bone. You be a good boy, hear?"

Pepperoni slurped a big kiss across Robert's hand.

When they had gone, Robert and his parents went back to the living room, where Charlie was rewinding the movie. "You missed some great scenes," he said.

"Oh, I wouldn't say that," said Robert's mom. Her voice sounded funny. Sure enough, her eyes were filled with tears.

Robert thought of Pepperoni as he had first seen him—just a skinny, neglected dog. Now Pepperoni was ready to live in a home where he would be loved. And he would never be far away from a pizza treat. It was time to let him go, and even his mom was sad.

"How are you doing, Tiger?" asked Robert's dad.

Surprised, Robert looked at his dad. His eyes weren't filled with tears, but he sounded sad, too.

They would all miss Pepperoni. But how could it have worked out any better? And maybe the next time he asked for a dog, his parents wouldn't say no so fast.

"I'm okay, Dad," he said. "I'm really okay."

67

BARBARA SEULING is a well-known author of fiction and nonfiction books for children, including several books about Robert. She divides her time between New York City and Vermont.

PAUL BREWER likes to draw gross, silly situations, which is why he enjoys working on books about Robert so much. He lives in San Diego, California, with his wife and two daughters.